DRAGONS
COLORING BOOK

Christy Shaffer

DOVER PUBLICATIONS, INC.
Mineola, New York

NOTE

Dragons are mythical creatures, often depicted as huge, scaly, serpent-like monsters, with wings, flaming breath and barbed tails. Found in many cultures around the world, dragons are generally regarded in the West as evil or malevolent, given to hoarding large sums of gold and jewels, and devouring fair maidens and hapless villagers who venture too close to their lairs. The dragons in the Old English epic poem *Beowulf,* and in the legend of St. George and the Dragon, are representative of this evil kind of dragon.

In the East, on the other hand, dragons are often seen as symbols of goodness, harmony and intelligence. Chinese dragons are thought to guard the homes of the gods, as well as controlling the weather and other earthly phenomena. Japanese dragons, known as *tetsu,* are able to change size at will, even to the point of becoming invisible. Eastern dragons can be identified by their number of toes: Chinese imperial dragons have five toes, four-toed dragons are Korean or Indonesian, while Japanese dragons possess three toes. Oriental dragons are often depicted with pearls in their mouths, under their chins or in their claws. The pearls symbolize the dragon's power and wisdom.

In this book you are invited to color 30 different kinds of dragons, ranging from the tiny, imaginary "fairy dragon," to such formidable real creatures as the giant lizard of Indonesia called the Komodo dragon. This is your opportunity to bring your own conceptions of color and hue to these fabulous creatures that have become so much a part of the world's mythology.

Bibliographical Note

Dragons Coloring Book is a new work, first published by Dover Publications, Inc., in 2002.

International Standard Book Number
ISBN-13: 978-0-486-42057-8
ISBN-10: 0-486-42057-4

Manufactured in the United States by RR Donnelley
42057417   2016
www.doverpublications.com

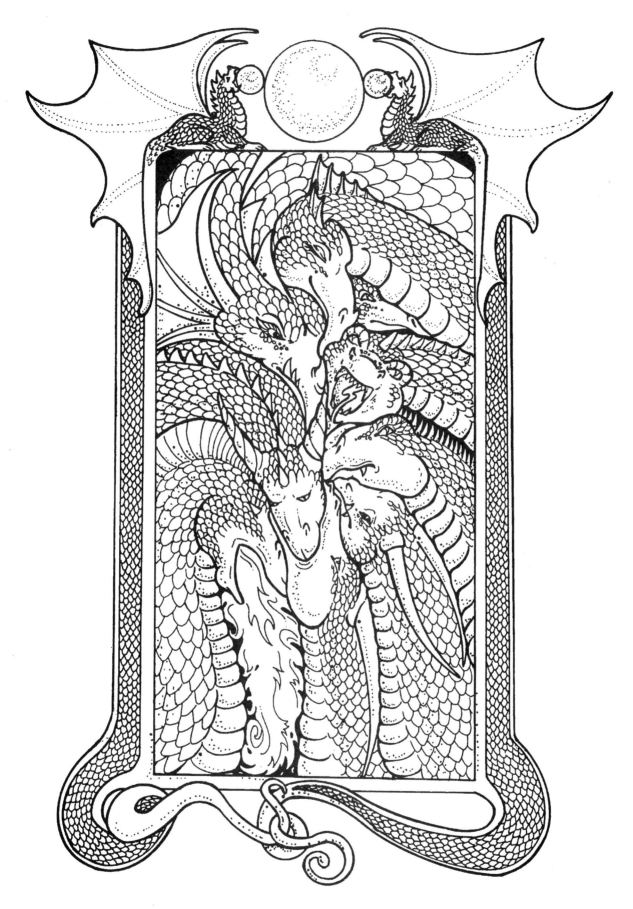

Dragons are imaginary creatures, represented as huge reptilian or saurian forms, with a crested head and scaly skin. Often, they possess wings and are shown breathing fire. Among the oldest mythological beasts, dragons appear throughout the world in almost every culture.

The wyvern's name is derived from the Anglo-Saxon word *wivere*, which means "serpent." These dragons have claws on their wings, as well as a poisonous stinger at the end of the tail.

Drakes are non-flying dragons that look like large lizards. There are two types: fire-drakes breathe fire and smoke, while cold-drakes breathe snow, ice and hail.

The cockatrice, or basilisk, was a legendary serpent endowed with a crest, or comb upon its head. Its glance was said to be lethal. The most effective way to destroy this creature was to show the cockatrice its own reflection in a mirror.

Beowulf is an Old English poem based on tales of a brave Scandinavian hero of the sixth century. Among many other feats, the warrior Beowulf kills a horrible monster known as Grendel that is devouring the soldiers of Hrothgar, King of Denmark. In his final battle, Beowulf slays a huge dragon before dying himself of a mortal blow.

Dragons with multiple heads are known as hydra. According to Greek mythology, when a hydra lost one head, two more would replace it. Slaying this particular dragon required burning the stump of the neck with a torch to keep the beast from regrowing its heads.

In England a young lord of Lambton went fishing one Sunday instead of going to church. He caught a hideous wormlike creature that he tossed into a local well. The young man then went off to fight in the Crusades. When he returned he found the huge dragon-like Lambton Worm terrorizing the village. Determined to kill the monster, the knight sought the advice of a witch, who told him to place spikes on his armor. While battling Sir Lambton, the dragon coiled around him and was pierced by the spikes, causing its death.

In Arthurian folklore, Merlin the wizard saw two huge dragons, one red and one white, locked in a fight to the death in a subterranean pool. The meaning of this, according to Merlin, was an omen of things to come, for the red dragon represented the Britons, and the white dragon, the Saxons, who would oppress the people of Britain. At first, the white dragon seemed to have the best of it, but then the red dragon drove the white one back.

10

The African amphisbaena was a very unusual dragon in that it had a head on each end of its body, allowing it to move swiftly in either direction. While guarding its nest, one head would watch over the eggs while the other head rested.

The amphitere was a legless serpent with multi-colored feathered wings and beautiful peacock-colored eyes. In Middle Eastern and European countries, this dragon was said to know all the world's secrets and to possess such powers as a hypnotic glance.

The mysterious and elusive fairy dragons are often mistaken for large butterflies or drag-onflies. They were favorite companions and mounts of the "wee people."

In South American legend, the quetzalcoatl is a large feather-covered serpent. This type of leg- less winged dragon is covered with brightly col- ored feathers as well as the traditional scales.

Fafnir, a greedy, evil sorcerer in Norse mythology, transformed himself into a monstrous dragon to guard his stolen treasure. The clever warrior Sigurd slew Fafnir by digging a pit near his water hole, rolling up under the dragon and stabbing the beast.

Mounted on a dragon high above France, the beautiful but dangerous spirit called *Le Succube* hunted for lovers. The kiss of *Le Succube* was deadly, however, for it drained the life from her unfortunate partners.

Marina, a Russian witch, kept a dragon and serpents in her palace as companions. She enjoyed seducing young warriors and changing them into creatures such as pigs or oxen. In the end, a clever knight tricked Marina into being alone with him, whereupon he beheaded her.

For years, the island of Rhodes was plagued by a terrible dragon. Knight after knight vowed to rid the island of this scourge, but none succeeded. Finally a knight named Dieudonne de Gozon made a life-size model of the dragon and trained two dogs and a horse to battle it. When the time was right, Sir Dieudonne and his animal companions attacked and killed the great beast.

Unable to satisfy a fierce dragon with sacrifices of sheep, a town instituted a lottery to choose human victims in hopes of appeasing the dragon. Saint George arrived at the town on the day that a princess was to be sacrificed. Saint George courageously attacked the dragon, killing it and saving the princess. To show their gratitude, the townspeople agreed to be baptized.

During his travels, the famous knight Sir Lancelot happened upon a French village where the people pleaded with him for help against an evil dragon. The knight went to the dragon's nest in a nearby tomb. After a long and terrible battle, Sir Lancelot slew the fearsome beast.

In China, dragons were considered beneficent creatures. They were believed to protect the heavens, watch over all gems, jewels and metals in the earth, command the weather, and control the flow and course of rivers. Chinese imperial dragons are recognized by the fact that they possess five toes. The fan tail of the dragon shown here marks her as a female.

Korean dragons differ from other Eastern dragons, because of their four toes and narrower faces.

These dragons frequently used pearls to help them acquire power or ascend into the heavens.

23

Oriental dragons, unlike Western ones, were not considered bad, but intelligent and good. Japanese dragons were called *tetsu* and had three toes. The knot tail signifies that this dragon is a male.

Shown here is a Polynesian underwater dragon called a Moo. Mainly known for its thieving ways, it is blamed by fishermen for missing items. In this case it has gotten away with a very large pearl.

Sightings of the Loch Ness monster in Scotland have been reported as far back as Saint Columba, a sixth-century Irish Legend has it that Saint Columba went on a boat and inscribed the sign of the cross in the air over the monster,

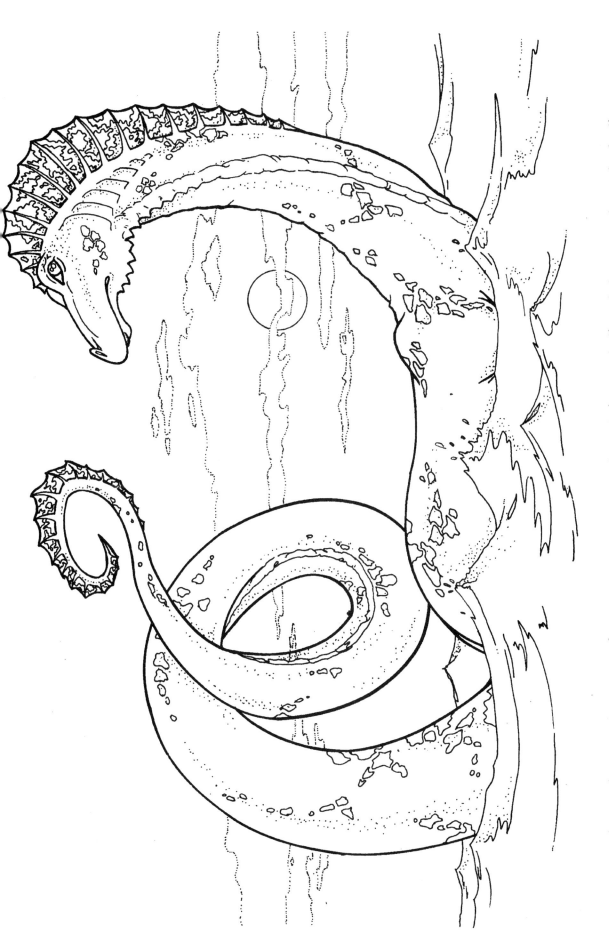

A leviathan is a sea monster of enormous proportions. Mentioned in the Bible, this fearsome creature ruled the oceans and destroyed ships that came too close. It is now believed that most legends dealing with leviathans are actually stories about whales.

The largest living lizard in the world, found only in Indonesia, is the Komodo dragon, which can grow up to ten feet long. This deadly predator not only has powerful claws and large, serrated teeth, its saliva is so toxic it will kill any animal the dragon bites, usually in less than a week.

The leafy sea dragon is a real animal, named for its similarity to the dragons of Chinese legend. Leafy sea dragons are found only in the waters off southern Australia. Camouflage is this creature's greatest weapon, allowing it to blend into the seaweed where it feeds on small shrimp.

Draco, or dragon, is a constellation of stars based on a Greek myth in which Heracles (Hercules) steals apples from a tree of gold guarded by Ladon the dragon. Heracles was forced to kill the dragon with poisoned arrows. Hera, Queen of the Gods, was so upset over the loss of Ladon, she placed his body in the sky in the form of a constellation.

30

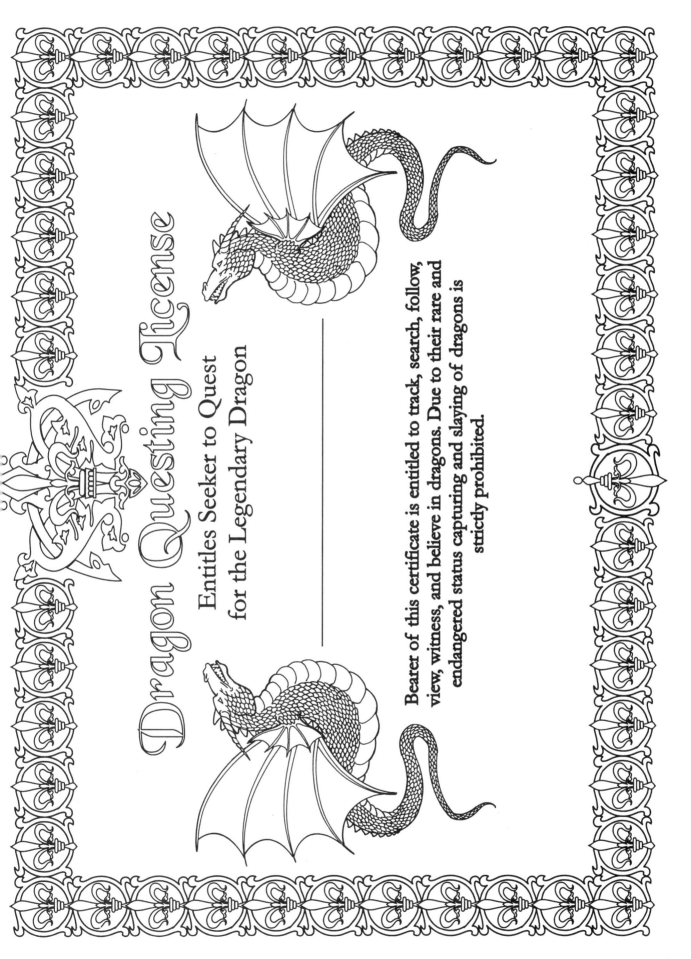

Dragon Questing License

Entitles Seeker to Quest
for the Legendary Dragon

Bearer of this certificate is entitled to track, search, follow, view, witness, and believe in dragons. Due to their rare and endangered status capturing and slaying of dragons is strictly prohibited.

Use your imagination to create a legendary dragon of your own. Add a background, scales, horns, spikes, wings, a rider or whatever you decide.